The Sun and the Wind

Written by Pippa Goodhart
Illustrated by Eva Montanari

Collins

One day the sun said to the wind,
"What shall we do for fun?"

The wind said, "Look at this."
He blew off a hat.

Then he blew off a bin lid.
Clang!

"Hats and bins are easy to
blow around!" said the sun.

A man came up the hill.

"I bet that *I* can blow off that
man's coat," said the wind.
"Look at this."

4

The sun hid in the clouds, and
the wind began to blow.
Huff-puff-puff.

"That's a chilly wind!" said
the man. He got his hood up.

The wind blew harder.
Huff-puff-puff-puff.

The wind was fresh and cool.
The man did up his coat.

"I bet I can beat you!" said the sun.
"I can get his coat off."

So the wind hid in the cloud and
let the sun have a go.

The sun came out, red hot.

"Such hot sunshine!" said
the man, and he took off his hood.

"Ha, ha!" said the sun.

The sun became hotter. The man
undid his coat.

"Hee, hee," said the sun.
"Soon that coat will be off!"

The sun got hotter and hotter.

"I'm far too hot!" said the man, and he took his coat off.

"Ha, ha, ha! Hee, hee, hee! I win!" said the sun.

"Well, I think that *I* am the winner!" said the man, with a smile.

"The wind will fly my kite,
and the sun is good for a picnic,"
said the man.

"Look at that," said the sun to the wind. "He is glad of us."

"We are a fantastic team," said the wind.

A fantastic team

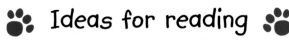

Ideas for reading

Written by Clare Dowdall, PhD
Lecturer and Primary Literacy Consultant

Learning objectives: *(reading objectives correspond with Yellow band; all other objectives correspond with Purple band)* recognise and use alternative ways of pronouncing graphemes; apply phonic knowledge and skills as the prime approach to reading unfamiliar words that are not completely decodable; draw together ideas and information from across a whole text; engage with books through exploring and enacting interpretations; present part of traditional stories for members of their own class

Curriculum links: Geography

Focus phonemes: ay, a-e, ea (beat), ee, y (ee), ew, ow (blow), oa, ou, igh, i-e, y (fly)

Fast words: to, the, who, said, to, what, we, do, are, have, he

Resources: ICT, paper, pencils, percussion instruments

Word count: 270

Getting started

- Revise the focus phonemes together and remind children that long vowel sounds are often made up of two or three letters (digraphs and trigraphs).

- Tell children that you're going to read a story that contains lots of words with long vowel sounds and that they will need to use their phonic skills to read them.

- Read the title and blurb with the children. Ask children if they know the story already. Ask them to look at the cover and predict what game the sun and the wind might play together.

Reading and responding

- Read the text on p2. Model reading from within the speech bubbles as well as the text and using different voices and appropriate expression for each character.

- Ask for two volunteers to read the text on p3 aloud. Choose one to be the narrator and one to be the sun. After reading, ask children to explain how the punctuation helps them, e.g. speech marks to show where speech begins and ends.